Copyright © 1995 by NordSüd Verlag AG, CH-8005 Zürich, Switzerland.
First published in Switzerland under the title *Die zertanzten Schuhe*.
English translation copyright © 1995 and 2010 by North-South Books Inc., New York 10016.
All rights reserved.
No part of this book may be reproduced or utilized in any form or by any means, electronic
or mechanical, including photo-copying, recording, or any information storage and retrieval system,
without permission in writing from the publisher.

First published in the United States, Great Britain, Canada, Australia, and New Zealand in 1995
by North-South Books Inc., an imprint of NordSüd Verlag AG, CH-8005 Zürich, Switzerland.
This edition first published in the United States, Great Britain, Canada, Australia, and New Zealand in 2013
by North-South Books Inc., an imprint of NordSüd Verlag AG, CH-8005 Zürich, Switzerland.

Distributed in the United States by NorthSouth Books Inc., New York 10016.

Library of Congress Cataloging-in-Publication Data is available.
A CIP catalogue record for this book is available from The British Library.
Printed in Germany by Grafisches Centrum Cuno GmbH & Co. KG, 39240 Calbe, January 2013.
ISBN 978-0-7358-4121-5 (trade edition)
1 3 5 7 9 • 10 8 6 4 2

www.northsouth.com

The Twelve Dancing Princesses

The Brothers Grimm · illustrated by Dorothée Duntze

North
South

Once upon a time there was a king who had twelve beautiful daughters.

Their beds stood side by side in a great room. Every night, after they went to bed, the king closed and locked their bedroom door. But every morning, when he opened it again, he found holes in their shoes. How it happened was a mystery.

One day the king proclaimed that any man who discovered how the princesses wore out their shoes every night could choose one of them for his wife and rule the country after the king's death. However, if he failed to solve the mystery after three nights, the man would be executed.

Before long a young prince came to try his luck. He was made welcome, and that evening he was given a room next to the princesses' bedroom. The door was left open so that the princesses could not do anything in secret or leave by any other way.

But the prince's eyes soon felt as heavy as lead, and he fell asleep. When he awoke in the morning, the twelve princesses' shoes were filled with holes again. The same thing happened on the second night, and again on the third, so without mercy the prince's head was cut off.

Many others came after him hoping to solve the riddle, but they all lost their heads as well.

One day a poor soldier who had been wounded in battle met an old woman on the road.

"Where are you going?" the old woman asked.

"I hardly know," said the soldier. "Though I wouldn't mind finding out how the king's daughters wear holes in their shoes and becoming king myself one day," he added as a joke.

"That's not as difficult as you might think," said the old woman. "Just don't drink the wine they bring you in the evening and pretend to be fast asleep." Then she gave him a cape and said, "If you put on this cape you will be invisible, and you can follow the princesses unseen."

The soldier took this good advice seriously. Plucking up his courage, he went to the palace and told the king he had come to seek the hand of one of the princesses in marriage. He was welcomed as hospitably as the other suitors and given royal clothes to wear.

That evening he was taken to the room next to the princesses' bedroom. As he was getting ready for bed, the eldest princess brought him a glass of wine. But the soldier had tied a sponge under his chin. He let the wine run into the sponge and did not drink a drop. Then he lay down and pretended to fall asleep.

When the princesses heard him snoring, they laughed. "There is another man who is tired of life!" said the eldest.

Then the princesses opened their chests and closets and pulled out
magnificent gowns and jewels and shoes. They dressed in front of their
mirrors, skipping about and laughing happily.

All except the youngest princess. "I feel very strange," she said, "though I don't know why. I'm sure some misfortune is about to happen."

"Silly goose," said the eldest princess. "You're always afraid of something. Don't you remember how many princes have already tried their luck and failed?"

When they were already, the princesses looked at the soldier. His eyes were closed and he was lying perfectly still, so they felt sure he was asleep.

Then the eldest princess went over to her bed and tapped it. It immediately sank into the floor, and the princesses climbed down through the opening one by one, led by the eldest.

The soldier, who had seen all this, wasted no time in putting on his cape and following the youngest princess. But halfway down the stairs, he stepped on her dress. She started in surprise. "What was that?" she cried. "Who is holding my dress?"

"Don't be silly," said the eldest princess. "You must have caught it on a nail."

They went all the way down the stairs. At the bottom was a wonderful avenue of trees with leaves made of shiny, glittering silver.

"I'd better take something back as proof," the soldier thought, and he broke off a twig from one of the trees. The tree gave a great crack.

"What was that?" the youngest princess cried again. "Did you hear that crack?"

But the eldest princess said, "That's just our princes firing shots of joy to salute us because we will soon have set them free from the spell."

Next they came to an avenue of trees with golden leaves, and finally to a third avenue with leaves made of sparkling diamonds. The soldier broke off a twig of gold and another of diamonds, and each time there was a crack that frightened the youngest princess. But the eldest insisted that the sounds were just a salute being fired to welcome them.

They went on until they came to a great lake where twelve little boats bobbed in the water. In each was a handsome prince. The princes had been waiting for the princesses, and each took one of them into his boat. The soldier got into the same boat as the youngest princess.

"I don't know why it is," said the prince, "but my boat seems much heavier tonight. It takes all my strength to make it move at all."

"It must be the warm weather," said the princess. "I feel the heat myself."

On the other side of the lake stood a beautiful castle, brightly lit and filled with the merry music of drums and trumpets.

The boats crossed the lake and everyone went into the castle, where each prince danced with his sweetheart. The invisible soldier danced too; and when one of the princesses had a goblet of wine in her hand, he would take it and drink the wine as she was raising it to her mouth. The youngest princess was frightened, but her eldest sister kept telling her not to worry.

They danced until three in the morning, when the princesses' shoes were
filled with holes and they had to stop. Then the princes took them back
across the lake. This time the soldier went first, with the eldest princess.

On the bank, the princesses said good-bye to their princes and promised
to come back the next night.

When they reached the stairs, the soldier ran on ahead, removed his cape, and lay down in bed. By the time the twelve princesses had climbed wearily up the stairs, he was snoring so noisily that they could all hear him. "We're safe enough from him!" they thought. They took off their beautiful gowns, put them away, placed their worn-out shoes under their beds, and went to sleep.

The soldier decided not to say anything yet. He wanted to see those strange sights again. So he went with the princesses on the second night, and the third too. Everything was just the same as it had been on the first night, and every night the princesses danced until their shoes were filled with holes. On the third night, though, the soldier brought away a goblet as further proof.

When the time came for the soldier to report to the king, he took along the three twigs and the goblet. The twelve princesses hid behind the door to hear what he would say.

"Well, where have my daughters been every night wearing holes in their shoes?" asked the king.

"Dancing with twelve princes in a castle underground," replied the soldier. Then he told the king all he had seen and showed his proofs. The king summoned his daughters and asked them if the soldier was telling the truth. Seeing that their secret had been discovered and there was no use in denying it, the princesses admitted to everything.

The king asked the soldier which princess he would choose for his wife.
"I'm not as young as I once was," said the soldier, "so give me the eldest."

The wedding was held that very day, and the soldier was promised the crown after the old king's death. But a magic spell was cast over the princes again, and it lasted as many days as they had spent nights dancing with the twelve princesses.